The Last Laugh

Copyright © Nick Voro 2024

All rights reserved. No part of this publication may be reproduced or transmitted in any form or by any means, electronic or mechanical, including photocopying, recording, or any information storage and retrieval system, without permission in writing from the publisher.

First Edition

The Last Laugh

VoroBooks, Etobicoke, Ontario, Canada

ISBN: 978-1-7777790-9-2

Typesetting and additional design by Lee Thompson Editing+

To contact the author: Nick_Voro@hotmail.com

This is a work of fiction. Names, characters, places and incidents either are products of the author's imagination or are used fictitiously. Any resemblance to actual events or locales or persons, living or dead, is entirely coincidental.

THE LAST LAUGH

I AM JUST GOING TO SAY THIS: rejection is tough to accept, tough to swallow, tougher still on unaccomplished rising stars, tough even on the toughest professionals, the risen stars, the accredited accomplished performers of stand-up comedy who to this day may still experience the occasional heckling, or booing, and feel rejection's venomous sting. No amount of preparation truly prepares you; no amount of bracing improves

Conversational Therapy

upon the impact of that prickling sensation. You do not get to walk away unscathed; be thankful you even get to walk away, unlike some of those greener newcomers.

The barbarianism of The Audience, an audience that can talk back. Have a voice of their own, even though they are not the ones up on stage holding the microphone. The pomposity of the enthroned performer. The delusional thought processes of the artistic mind. Thinking he can evade the menacing eyes, escape the mounting tension of expectation, standards set skyscraper high in that opulent room. Wanting to prove them wrong, win them over, conquer and convert those witnesses to his highs and lows. Laughter, the lifeblood of any comedian. Attainment of praise. Receiving tabloidal recognition. A cushioned performance. A great success! Menacing faces unmasked, the room flooding with humanness, projecting back reassurances to the comedian on stage, knowing now with certainty that he has converted them, that they are his, their deafening

The Last Laugh

applause is for him, that it all belongs to him from now on, the clapping, the cheering, the admiration, idealization, his kind of crowd, avowing to follow him, the comedic Messiah to the very end, to his final farewell performance.

And this is exactly how it was for the longest time until the slippage. Then came the rejection. The tough to accept rejection. Even tougher without a proper explanation. Like a lover departing without so much as leaving a farewell note. Deafening silence replaced the applause. Lackluster attendance followed. The Audience even lacked energy needed for the usually charged heckling and booing. They just got up from their seats and left the room. The venues changed; opulence replaced with decrepitude. Soon the appointment book was wide open, unimpeded with scheduled or unscheduled performances. I retreated to my condominium; security afforded through amassment of funds from previous more successful shows. Confined to a catacomb, none the wiser as to the reason. It bothered me. The reason. Engulfed in

Conversational Therapy

the unknown. Harboring resentment at the lack of clarity, forever living with the remembrance of those unmuzzled barbarians letting me know exactly what they think. Unable to forget the sensation of dampness, my clothes drenched, doused in their critique. Unfortunately, not a very in-depth critique since I never did learn the reasoning behind their rebellion. Simply capitulating to their demands, the demands of the audience, signing the contract signaling my immediate retirement from the stage, from holding the microphone with a firm grip. Betraying my artistic roots. And once I finished and put down the pen, they did not so much as offer a thank you. No commiseration from that mob. It is as if this is exactly how it should have been all along. The beckoning hand of the butchers, ready to slaughter you. One guillotine reserved for the unamusing comedian.

This sanction, this sacking of my long-built career, can hardly be considered an inconsequential event. It is anything but that. A dreadful

The Last Laugh

development. A magnitudinous setback. Living a meaningless existence, grievous over what once was. In the absence of a career, that feeling of excitation disappears. Everything joyous disappears. What remains is the horrible immensity of time on one's hands. To live with oneself. Split responsibilities of performer and spectator. Most unnatural to a comedian, a performer, accustomed to being projected onto the lives of others. And I know what you are going to say, so spare me. Pain takes time to heal. Don't I know it. Don't we all know it? The problem is, when there is just so much of it, you begin putting up fences, boarding yourself up from the rest of the world while wallowing in severe depression, trying to reach out to others for help while not coming to terms with the real issue. Acceptance of the current reality as the only real way of stopping the cycle of self abuse. The hinderance of heightened emotionalism. Depleted, I felt revulsion toward the world at large, nothing to rouse me from this torpor. I committed the worst sin known to a performance art-

Conversational Therapy

ist. I slowed down. Even unwanted, I could have kept creating, kept writing, each joke repudiating their ruling. Instead I entered this paralytic state, lodging there, registered as a dissuaded artist/dead artist in the reservation logbook. Having done about the worst thing a person can do to themselves. And I remained there, waiting. But waiting for what?

In this concocted state I bereaved my career, too incurably embittered to see some semblance of light at the end of the dark tunnel. Some glimmer of hope. A cavernous hole formed deep inside my chest. Compelled to close this opening, I resolved to using food, a poor substitute in hindsight, as a stand-in for bricks to cover the passage. Patching this hole did not expunge the void accompanying me wherever I went. In an almost masochistic fashion, in the course of time, I stopped worrying; I became enthralled, captivated with this chosen for me calamitous path. I went along, barred myself from the outside world living inside of my monastic retreat. Revelling in my reckless

The Last Laugh

pursuit, consuming mammoth portions of comestibles. A guttural gluttony of everything under the sun. A complete wipeout trying desperately as a last resort to lessen the internalized pain, trying to escape the inescapable memories of uncongested rooms, unobliging audience, stationary hands of the unenthused crowd refusing vigorous clapping, refusing a standing ovation.

Excessive weight-gain followed. What did I expect from a stultified stationary existence spent in a swivel chair? Combine this with the refrigerator and all its unprotected provisions so close, just a few push-offs away, and you have a disaster in the making, the steaming cauldron, the Witches' Brew from Macbeth. What started out as a harmless pastime naturally progressed to something more sinister, spiralling out of my control, innumerable insatiable intakes, administering everything I could get my hands on down my esophagus, simply unmanageable by someone who lacked self-control, was weak-willed, with arms that should have been straight-jacketed.

Conversational Therapy

I was constantly a victim to this animalistic hunger, these rippling pangs, this insufferable ravenousness, always there, always looming above, encircling from all sides, triggering, provoking, driving me into a corner where I crouched, curled up, defeated and completely powerless. This weight gain, this excessive blubber, came to define me. Not so much a rough patch, more like my life in a nutshell. It took some time to accept this fact, that when I go to bed, I am not going to wake up in the morning any skinnier, maybe even bigger, making that weight scale needle climb higher and higher until it has no place to go.

This predisposition to weight fluctuations always existed, a regrettable inheritance courtesy of my parents. I rallied and fought hard against it in my younger years. The formative years. The only fighter in my family, really. But once I reached some level of cognizance, all hope withered away. With this newfound clarity I started to understand the root problem with my family, the true underlying causes behind my weight gain

The Last Laugh

outside the diminished MC4R gene, the fact that no one in it had any heart or a soul. My father tuned everything anyone said to a low frequency his old police scanner would not even pick up. A once great man, retired from the force after more than thirty years of service, helping people left and right. But at home, he could not even listen to his own children or wife's demands. My mother, on the other hand, had a nasty habit of getting behind the wheel of our old beat-up van and driving away whenever emotions struck her. An unfulfilled woman, constantly enervated, easily spooked, unequipped to deal with high intensity situations, like the daily squabbles between her and her husband, she tried to salvage what she could of herself, what parts remained, and in this she would find no opposition from anyone else, this was hers and hers alone. Hardly an idyllic household. Intermittent tremors rattled the foundation, caused by unsticking of once deadlocked familial bonds, shaking the established stronghold housing two adults and four children. It is

Conversational Therapy

always fascinating to return, to leaf through that old family album, to elucidate your childhood experiences from a more mature perspective, provide commentary with insights to painful events eluded in childhood.

It is not surprising I turned out how I did. A damaged outcast who thought for a long time that his life was not going anywhere.

I do apologize, dear reader; I do not mean to sound self-dramatizing. But I do think there is plenty to scrutinize in our past, the precursor to countless individuals' defective maturation, stunting the growth, causing irreparable damage to the mind. Specialists cite improper handling from the very beginning, mishandling of the young impressionable mind. Very much like my own at the time of my testimony. So please, allow me to continue, to bring you to my level, where you will gain knowledge and understanding as to the function and purpose of each individual cog in the mechanism, the inner-workings of me. Allow me to unburden myself.

The Last Laugh

As I was saying, these people, this so-called family, flattened my expectations. The effects are still present, still settling like dust in a recently vacuumed room. A reminder of pain's immortality. Pain that still wanted very much to undermine, ambush, breach the fortified fort I relentlessly spent so much time strengthening, hoping it would prove resilient during subsequent attacks. Pain that remained. Engaged in a never-ending assailment. Storming the fort, with me constantly repairing the damage to the walls.

I can still recall the inconsiderable favoritism. Only choosing to love those they understood, those whose emotional problems they could solve easily. Never for a moment contemplating the damaging effects bestowed upon the youngest child through these tactics. The seldom care, something that should have been a birthright. My siblings were the true beneficiaries, while I faced unremitting besiegement.

Time passed, my parents held on to their ways, unable to relinquish, remaining incorrigible,

Conversational Therapy

no room left in their lives for ideas about self-betterment and generally better parenting. These were older people, set in their ways, non-conformist and non-pliant. Custodians from the underworld, and I the sacrificial lamb. My mother began disappearing more and more frequently, trying to locate a haven for her drinking problem and compensate for the love she was not getting at home with strangers she met on the wide-open road (or the parking lot of the nearest bar). My father, the heavily inebriated bum, mostly watched telly, guzzling down the contents of the "next" can of beer without so much as a comment, nervously running his hand through his thinning hair and only getting up to stumble to the bathroom, usually leaving behind a sprinkling of scaly skin on the floor. He never lost his grip on the drink; it was his mind eventually checking out on a leave of absence that caused him to become incommunicado for days at a time, trading his insignia of ill-humor for psychopathic lashing-out, usually with a belt, buckle side to buttocks,

The Last Laugh

back and sometimes face. A tuned-out tyrant terrorizing his own helpless child, unresponsive to any number of imploring pleas and nightmarish screams.

I spent most of my adolescent life wishing I were dead, so all the pain collected over the years would go away, and I would not have to wake up and face a living hell. This is around the time my eating disorder developed, not that anyone in my family bothered to notice that anything was wrong with me.

Then came the suicide attempt that got everyone's attention, my fifteen minutes of fame with my own family, although even then, they did not say much about it, unable to comfort, to express, to feign care beyond shock and surprise. To draw from a tank with an insufficient supply of emotional empathy. Foreigners to my feelings. I take that back. One family member did have something to say. My oldest sister Sandra said, "I guess I have to call poison control now," after discovering me spread out on a bathroom floor,

Conversational Therapy

having washed down Tylenol with carpet cleaner. It was her boyfriend's birthday too, so she was especially angry with me. I do not remember much except the emergency room, the one therapy session, being discharged and being prescribed anti-depressants, which I thought I would be taking for the duration of this life and the next.

The saving grace of the matter was not having to worry about how my parents felt. Apathetic, sighing, pronouncing this as mere acting out, sweeping it speedily under the rug. No attempts made to deal with their fear-stricken child. Emotional responsiveness would not be prised from these people. A pair of warped characters, perceiving suicide as a trivial matter, alumnus and alumna of the old school teachings: some things are better left unsaid. Talking perceived as a sure sign of weakness, especially with the least liked family member, inviting vulnerability, surrenderment of self to verbal communication with a nauseating nuisance, a misbehaving little vulgarian.

How I craved the naturalness of normalcy, a

The Last Laugh

normative family dynamic. To nab the spotlight occasionally. To have a chance to stray from my permanent state of quietude. Engage in conversations, practice communication, have a proper outlet for my self-expression. I had a whirlpool of opinions. Unfortunately, all brushed aside. I felt like I did not exist at all. When hatred replaces love, it can be a stimulant that motivates you to succeed in the eyes of those who want your downfall.

Since my declarative gesture went unnoticed, unable to reassert my presence, remind them of my existence, convince them of our connectivity, all those failed attempts, I decided to renounce them, end the cycle of abuse, reconstitute my life, a fresh start, follow in my mother's footsteps and salvage something, hopeful the rescued piece proved sizeable enough to help me build upon and guarantee anything other than placement on a dirty stool of the local watering hole, dismantling my stress through drink, downturned lips realigning themselves to a would-be smile just to take

Conversational Therapy

the next poisonous sip, then returning to the previous state, unofficially undertaking the role of a describer of all faults with the world, desperately trying to convince anyone who would listen how terminal life is.

I wanted hope. A hope for the future. So, I moved out. There were no exaggerated theatrical partings, no severance of speaking terms for they did not exist, just a forfeiture of family ties for a clean slate. I packed my life away in a few duffle bags and left. This perfectly-timed escape emboldened me to tackle the world. Speculative prospecting followed, dead-end jobs, rental struggles, until sometime later, down the road of maturation and encountered disappointments, I decided I wanted to become a comedian. Cheaper than any therapist, and what better profession to channel your anger and still receive a steady paycheck. A chance to be the center of attention, lights flooding the stage, a packed venue, all eyes on one man with a microphone, a humorist parading in front of them; the live audience, an

The Last Laugh

entertainer purposely acting like a poppycock, a medieval period court jester time-travelled to a modern-day comedy club. Sure, it might seem contrived, automated, writing and telling jokes to benefit others, needing their approval, their rating, but eventually you get to take the reins and do for "self" what you have been doing for "others." And this starts with a single moment. You will know when it comes. That pivotal moment, the big win, a moment of pure artistry, incremental changes beginning to take place from one home-run-landed joke, so paramount to a comedian's success, a stroke of luck when your painstakingly prepared material wins them over. You start seeing a suffusion of smiles, bustling about originating from pure excitement, pure magic, opening of barricaded doors, dissolvement of the barrier between performer and the audience, you gain ability to cross over becoming one of them, nested, chosen, part of a family you never had.

You gain the ability to write for yourself, please yourself foremost, while still being swarmed by

Conversational Therapy

adoring fans. I was meant to play this role. And play it perfectly. I was a natural. It all came so easily. Almost second nature. I suppose it helped to grow up surrounded by unswayable Neanderthals, disheartened and hostile, impossible to please. The dysfunctional household where I planted the seeds for future career harvest. A practice run for the toughest-to-please club audiences on my comedic pilgrimage.

And when they stop laughing at your jokes? Is that what you are asking, dear reader? Well, you know all about that already. Which brings us right around again, back to the present. The inescapable present. Where I find myself reading an invitation to perform in the party room of my condominium. A thirty-minute set. First gig, first opportunity in almost three years. A rupture in the routine, weaning from mundaneness. Summonses of success. That fleeting second chance up for grabs. A precious opportunity for career resurrection. No, an advantageous opportunity for a confrontation, the jilted lover

The Last Laugh

accosting their former romantic partner, accruing insight, enlightenment, an explanation for the change of heart. Although, I instantly foresee a problem. With my niche interest in ingestion of food, immense amounts of it, I have gained considerable poundage; instead of having far-flung interests, I zeroed in, focusing obsessively until I found myself in a perilous state, worshipping a temptress, and as a long-term tenant in her temple, I would have to break the lease.

I cringed at the idea, simultaneously noticing my shirt had a covering of crumbs, in addition to being decorated with patterns of sweat embroidery. I could feel them now, sweat rivulets lubricating my useless limbs, nailed to my swivel chair, itching terribly, thinking about this uncooperative body of mine. I had to start reshaping my thought patterns, and I was more than willing to tackle the toilsome task of standing up for the carrot-invitation dangling before me, although, the actuality of implementing my thoughts within the realm of reality was a bit

Conversational Therapy

more difficult, to move those immobile feet, tear through that tremendous enjoyment those feet felt of true inactivity, feet with slight archness to them enjoying surface comfortability of a wool-silk blend of a great Persian carpet.

Yes, a true natural at wasting time, completely in my element. My body a blunt tool, a symbol opposing optimal fitness, my mouth when not occupied with large quantities of food issuing declarative statements, protestations against progressive pedestrians with quick nimble feet and ability to keep a steady pace. Enough! Enough idling. I looked above, greeted at once by the sturdy metallic handle suspended overhead, lonesome and anticipating the reaching hand, a handle attached to a length of galvanized wire rope attached in-turn to a set of heavy-duty wheels on a ceiling mounted movable track tracing the interior of the condominium, not at all dissimilar to a pulley system, albeit reconfigured, improved upon and able to hold upwards of four hundred pounds.

The Last Laugh

I fastened my fingers around the handle, getting on with the programme. I tugged mightily; it held; a system holding strong, manufacturer's promise upheld, a system working exactly as it should, a dependable continuous source of support reassuring me I had not exceeded the weight limit. Wheezing, I launched myself to a standing position. Severest punishment to my body. It is noteworthy to say that my task seemed a tad bit easier imagined than the implementation at hand now: a treacherous journey beyond the kitchen and the stainless-steel refrigerator. I blinked, took a step, then another, a sequence of footsteps, beginnings of acceleration, footsteps thundering, floorboards creaking, my eyes watering. I looked down at my shirt, it looked ridiculous, crumpled with accordion folds, a victimized article of clothing of unwanted undesired staining due to my overactive sweat glands. Avant-garde men's dress code: a crinkled and sweat-drenched shirt?

And here was good old peripheral vision doing its job, intercepting, even though I tried so hard to fixedly stare ahead, to evade the monolith, a

Conversational Therapy

skyscraper casting its long shadow, internalized since childhood, an adolescent sentimental association, a timeless shadow on that dirty kitchen wall. My miniature hand reaching for the handle. From its towering perspective I must have seemed like one more kneeling worshipper, no identity, blending in, blindly bowing down before this seraphic being. Yes, it threw a heavy shadow and left a permanent mark. Etching itself on my subconscious mind. A place of permanence. An uninvited guest that just would not leave. Even now I could envision the vast richness of its interior, beyond the impenetrable vault door only granting access to those bestowed with the safe combination. Camouflaged behind the state-of-the-art security, combination-based lock, and vault door with sliding bolts, an opportunity for self-abandonment. No restrictions. Unbridled freedom. Rise to impulsivity. Riotous behavior.

Unethical thoughts entered my mind, chipping away at my brittle foundation. The apparatus began to glow with luminous intensity; all

The Last Laugh

the while my inquisitive mind could not resist fantasizing, craving a sugar-sweetened beverage, or a powder puff pastry sprinkled generously with sugar, to open the door and spot the familiar trustworthy Big Chill emblem with the name written in hieroglyphic font.

I craved a treat for my valiant efforts. I wanted it so much I knew I could not have it. Knowing perfectly well it would never be just one. I would never be able to consume just one. One would never be enough to solidify my nerves on my Don Quixote journey to the party room of my condominium building. I sighed. My feet picked up pace again. I was rebelling against my cravings. Denial. Denial which triggered a remembrance. An episodic recollection, pouncing on me. A postcard from the past. Two dots blinking on an interconnected graph of pain. She was on my mind again. What started as a mere thought shortly molded into a character sketch, a contour drawing with overlaying multitudinous lines, until a facial composite emerged. Her face,

Conversational Therapy

the face that gave me lifelong restlessness.

Who was she you might ask? Once upon a time, when I weighed a hundred and thirty pounds, I had a slightly overweight girlfriend. A good-natured person who fell for me, and who knows, maybe I would have fallen for her if it was not for that one minor problem. To me at the time, it was her only inferior quality, making her incomplete in my eyes. One step away from perfection, and madly in love with me. What was I to do as a selfish, pitiful creature that I was? I broke her heart, unable to give her what she sought after—the return of affection.

No kind words were a substitute for her pain; niceties do not equal compensation when you break someone's heart. Before we parted ways, I remember she asked me if I found her attractive. I replied that I did not because she was much bigger than I would have preferred. It is funny how weight, like extra emotional baggage, can keep you from loving someone. But it does; there is no denying it.

The Last Laugh

Trust me, dear reader, I know what you are thinking. And you are right. I learned about unconditional love, compromise, and reality of living a tad bit too late, way after being diagnosed with irregular levels of cholesterol and suffering through and surviving my first heart attack. She was already long gone.

At that time, I was a student of media-promoted negative body image, allowing society to spoon feed me, consumerism consuming me. I denied someone a part of me because I was merely a product of superficiality, chasing after the wrong things, letting her slip away. And after my fall from fame, I will never forget the sobering words someone said to me when I gained the first hundred pounds, "Welcome to the real-world asshole... no one thinks you are the life of the party. You are not the greatest gift bestowed upon humanity; just another fat bastard..."

Now isolated within these concrete confines, I cannot help but reminisce and contemplate what could have been. In a cruel twist of fate, I

Conversational Therapy

was what I once rejected. Continuously sliding down an endless slope. Stranded in downward motion, possessor of a single move, resigned to my spiral of poisonous thoughts, a torturous reprise. Complete loss of control over my life, failure to remember the last time I had a good day. And it all started before the audience stopped laughing. It started when I lost her.

I reached the phone, dialing two numbers, one to confirm my comeback performance tonight, and the other, her number which had not changed in years. She accepted the invitation with a slightly quivering voice. My own throat constricted when I heard her voice, turning on the valves, tear ducts nearly flooding my condominium. I was extra nervous now, seeing her tonight after all this time and the audience's reaction to my weight gain. I would have to prepare accordingly. Naturally, there were expectations for me to do some of my old material. It made sense; they booked me on what little weight my name still carried in this industry. They were paying a

The Last Laugh

tribute, homage to the past; I was a throwback, a dinosaur, hardly a modernist trying to modernize the world. But I did have a surprise in-store for them. A single self-referential joke, making fun of my own asinine hilariousness, therefore anticipating my attacker's advancing movements and checkmating him into a corner. I wanted to dismantle the governing body, The Audience, with a singular punchline securing my place, proving them wrong, a legacy left untarnished.

Do you think me excessive? You think things have changed. Sure, the world constantly changes, certain conversational topics become old and obsolete with time; fatness is not one of them. Still a rapidly circulating conversational piece. The society we are all part of is really a merciless jury that is trying awfully hard to ridicule and disprove of you. Sure, it is simple-mindedness and a part of what I like to call 21st-century ever-so-growing ignorance, but that is just how it is. I cannot blame them, I used to be one of them, it would take a lengthier period for things to truly

Conversational Therapy

change, and in the meantime, I have to prepare to deflect their criticism, to come up with the perfect joke, the most perfect punchline directly tackling all my critics all at once. The perfect retort. My magnus opus. Right in the center of all my work. An astounding similarity to my inebriated father's favourite inebriated writer's plans for his magnus opus, "The Voyage That Never Ends," a summation of all his life's work, with his masterpiece novel, *Under the Volcano*, as the centerpiece.

Confronting your critics is hardly a conventional method of gaining acceptance. But if done with finesse, a delicate balance of comedy and slice-of-life commentary, laughter if gained, would bring it all together, a key ingredient to softening the blow. Instead of being a clichéd angry comic firing back, you would rise to celebrity status for your ingenuity, celebrated for your extraordinary wit, having chosen the experimental, bypassing the more familiar.

This is what I was banking on. One joke to change the course of my personal history of

The Last Laugh

recent failures. A man possessed. In my last-ditch effort, inevitably heading toward self-destruction, or stardom. The rope suddenly stopped moving. I found myself standing before my front door. A milestone, but also the end of my assisted acceleration. From here on I would have to fend for myself, using walls or anything else I could hold onto.

Out in the hallway, my thoughts went back to The Audience. It was a suicide mission to take them on. In my state of decrepitude, overweight and aging ungracefully, to take on a room full of people, no singular opponents, no one-on-one battles, a whole slew of them. I knew what awaited me once I stepped onto that stage, it was always the same, at the beginning of every act, always a friendly expression on their faces and a slight touch of a devilish glimmer in their eyes, indicating to me as a comedian that if I slipped, found myself wounded and bleeding profusely, they would shred me to pieces without so much as a hint of mercy. The Audience anxiously awaits

Conversational Therapy

such a moment to strike you down. Each laugh is a confirmation of the fact that you fit in; each silent reaction, a sigh, or a boo, shoves you further in life's trash receptacle as a defective human being, an unworthy performer.

My raspy wheezing filled the hallway. I could tell my body was on the fritz, starting to malfunction. I had shortness of breath, a pair of struggling lungs and a birthing sensation of a fatal cough trying to claw its way out of my throat. Can you blame me for passing up the double-helix stairwell? The only condominium building around these parts with one, drawing inspiration from French Renaissance and Da Vinci's own creation for Château de Chambord. Nice to look at, but a royal pain in the arse to one's ascent or descent.

The elevator arrived timely, greeting me with a dinging noise and another plaque, this time an Elevator Capacity Plate, also in a hieroglyphic font identical to my Big Chill refrigerator.

The doors closed; the apparatus began descending, the steel cable did not snap, there was

The Last Laugh

no plummeting below for the single overweight occupant. I watched transfixed as floor numbers lit up, and grew dark, and lit up again, a zigzagging pattern, thinking about how I would amend the personal history of my historic failures, rewrite whole sections, modified to my liking, about the audience's receptivity below.

I always had this theory. That people who come to watch a comedy show, or any show for that matter, are simply individuals intensely combating the awkward silences in their lives. Silence that sneaked into their lives over time. A handful of years. Once the honeymoon period ended, their compatibility was suddenly tested, purposive hurt introduced to the loving relationship, from civilized to aggressive, caffeinated caged and shouting, shrieking and violent, craving reconciliation sex, riding that carousel more times they cared to discuss, until one day they just lost their zest for the whole thing, giving in, giving up, settling for marital unhappiness, responsibilities of raising children and mundaneness of

Conversational Therapy

everyday life. These people felt alone even when they were together. They wanted noise-cancelling headphones for their home life, white noise for the stinging and invading pain. They were way past talking to each other, trying, putting in the time and effort, past exchanging ideas, discussing vast topics ranging from corrupt politicians, inflating prices, city workers going on strike, whose marriage was falling apart due to yet another infidelity. No, these individuals have had their fill. They depleted the resources of communication amongst themselves. It no longer offered excitation. They wanted a tryst, a midnight rendezvous, to be tongue-tied for an evening, not having to worry about puritanical appearances, acceptable behavior, placing place settings and feeding their children with cherubic faces. Trading paradisiacal palisades of their guarded community, the spiritless suburbia for subterranean devilry. These were philistines, not patrons of the arts. They merely wanted escapism. A stranger to fill their heads. A morally corrupt stand-up comic

The Last Laugh

delivering the goods: immorality, immodesty, and obscenity. Food for thought, nutritive to their stale lives. Perhaps something they could even discuss behind locked doors, back in the privacy of their safe, secure homes.

Anyway, it is just a theory.

You know, doing stand up all these years, something I never got used to were the establishments themselves. A common reoccurring problem with most comedy clubs is the outdated décor, derivative patterns, overlapping and mismatched colors, an interior designer's disastrous vision, inverted measurements, and absence of spatial balance. Let us not forget excessive lighting, powerful projectors providing more than efficient illumination, enough light for you to be able to see gathering moisture on the performer's face and the fine layers of dust floating through the air which makes you self-consciously review if there is enough clean air in this facility in the first place to even breathe. Those dust collecting red theater curtains certainly did not help, placed there purely

Conversational Therapy

for the sake of adding that bit of theatrical flair. Particulate matter and incinerating lights, yes, those I could do without. The rest, I missed terribly. The venues being crowded and compressed with people, a myriad of servers zigzagging about with drink trays, camera crews capturing crystal clear moving images, a self-contained world unlike any other that does not stop spinning until the comedian on stage starts performing.

Tonight's venue could not be more different. On the plus side, the décor was not as atrocious, and there was sterility to the air. Unfortunately, it was also missing all the things I fondly described above. This was after all the party room of a condominium building, not an actual comedy club, a scaled-down version meant to accommodate a smaller audience with makeshift curtains and no camera crews. This comeback would be spread by word of mouth, hopefully still leading to greater business opportunities.

After spending some time waiting for my cue—allowing me time to jot down my joke—

The Last Laugh

they finally called for me. The foray toward the microphone was comprised of slow, deliberate steps. In my peripheral vision, I could see their eagerness growing. An inhospitable taste permeated my mouth, my muscles twitched; I had my repellent against their cynicism ready in the pocket of my dirty sweatpants, sanctuary to sweat-stained scribbles with the faultless joke. I imagined myself stripped bare before this lawless authority, suppressing a secret weapon, safeguarding these scraps, biding my time until I can reveal them, unveiling them at the moment of least expectation, catching The Audience completely off guard. Just before they display their jagged teeth, showing me the emotional poverty of humanity. The Emptiness. The Imbecility. Before they can entertain themselves with their own howling, crude amusement gained from taunting the performer. The people's government, the giant pressing machine flattening dissidents, operated by primitive peasants, shadowing my every action in anticipation of delivering repeated

Conversational Therapy

blows on behalf of the simple-minded society they represent; hoping and praying that the final heavy attack to my undersides will do the job of hemorrhaging my heart.

The air suddenly did not feel so sterile, more so tampered with, stifling and suffocating. I would have gritted my teeth if my jaw were not so tightly clenched. The audience's incessant chatter amongst themselves deafened me. A myriad of murmuring heads. And those unbearable lights, obliterating visibility, blinding my organ of sight. Mucus steadily ran toward the corners of my tightly interwoven lips. I skimmed the room for the last time with my hypersensitive eyes. So much pain had assembled within me. I was bursting. So much that on some level it was liberating to just give in. To cease fighting and embrace this pain. Handing myself over. Relinquishing. This room was my reliquary preserving my remains.

I felt a spreading pain, a series of spasms that brought me to a standstill, I was doing my best to be the receiver of this unconventional gift,

The Last Laugh

but was it a gift or a curse? I felt a pressure. I felt deformed, defeated, and drained. It was near impossible to generate new, or conserve old energy. A severe subtraction of fully functional organs. I feebly attempted to articulate my distress, gesticulating with my hands, but to no avail. The human factor in those seats showed no remorse, occupying their thrones with obscene comments right on the tips of their protruding tongues, recalled and retrieved just in time to accompany my staggering and struggling. Things had come full circle for me. I was staring directly at a freshly dug grave. Earth excavated in my honor. My final resting place. The microphone serving as a burial marker. The best funeral photographer in the business snapping away during the open-casket funeral service, capturing expertly the funereal pallor on my embalmed face. Colonnade of pallbearer's hands extended above their heads, moving centipede-like, transporting my casket.

I stared at them defiantly. These representatives of a world that has failed to comprehend

Conversational Therapy

my genius pulverizing me with their eyes. I poised myself, aware that these might be my last spoken words, a culmination of a comedian's career, a few relevant words of lasting importance. My joke. The set-up and punchline.

[Dear Readers: Please Insert Joke Here]

After the punchline, I remained still for what seemed to me an eternity. Then a misstep followed, a slip, spattering the stage with my convulsing body. Sprawled. Guilty of public littering. I suddenly had an inordinate desire to see the summits of holy mountains, hopeful the soaring heights would ward off the evil below. Sadly, I was not in optimal climbing condition, having reached the lowest of the lows, the stage floor. I could not possibly get any lower and death was steadfastly approaching. My time was up. The pied piper was calling my name. This was the price I had to pay. Myocardial infarction claiming me after years of service as a dedicated overeater.

I once went to a photographer. He looked me in the eyes and said, "You could look at the

The Last Laugh

devil with these and not even blink." I was looking at them now, The Audience, the clamorous mob, unblinking. The room erupted, a Roman amphitheatre vibrating with customary clapping and cheering mixed with bloodcurdling screams for paramedics. The Audience was devoid of a matching reaction. While I was desperate for uniformity, seeking assurances, substantive evidence, a revolutionary reaction of identicalness, a phenomenon like no other. The lack of balance tremendously tormented me. I began to drift off, still lacking the fundamental knowledge so important in deducing the source of their laughter, my joke, or my second this-time-possibly-fatal heart attack.

ABOUT THE AUTHOR

A native of Kyiv, Ukraine, but living in Canada since the age of eleven, Nick Voro discovered literature at an early age, never quite mustering the ability to put an excellent book down. A recent graduate of the Toronto Film School, Nick divides his time between being a full-time parent and a full-time author.

His debut work, *Conversational Therapy: Stories and Plays*, has recently sold over 200 copies and is part of the library system (United States, Canada, New Zealand, Australia and Scotland).

Lee D. Thompson, an editor and writer from Moncton, New Brunswick, Canada, edited this short story. His books include: a novel in [xxx] dreams from Broken Jaw Press, Mouth Human Must Die from Frog Hollow Press and Apastoral: A Mistopia from Corona/Samizdat. His short fiction has been published in many anthologies, including Random House's Victory Meat, New Fiction from Atlantic Canada and Vagrant Press's The Vagrant Revue of New Fiction. He is the winner of the David Adams Richards Prize (2018) and New Brunswick Book Award (2022). He is the publisher of Galleon Books.

Printed in the USA
CPSIA information can be obtained
at www.ICGtesting.com
CBHW071815060824
12792CB00056B/1106

Acknowledgements:

Thanks to the following magazines where these poems first appeared:

The Ragged Raven Press "The Ramifications of Knowing"
By-Line Magazine "Not Written by Candlelight"
Mastodon Dentist "The Perfect Picture" and "The River That Carries"
The Temenos Review "Having Spent My Time"
JAWS Magazine "Up-State Trying to Hold Onto What's Left of My Left Atrium" and "Shaking Trees to Loosen Leaves"
Flesh "Pavlov's Dogs"
Blind Man's Rainbow "Spider-Webbed Streetlights" and "The Words I Owe"
Arabesques Review "Gently Confused Smile" and "Things That Need a Second"

and to all the professors and friends who helped me to put this collection together.

Note:
In "The Cherry Blossoms are Blossoming" the lines "…the trees are screaming, / losing their minds, making beauty / and throwing it away." is from Tony Hoagland's poem "A Color of the Sky".